Rutherford B. Who Was He?

Poems About Our Presidents

Marilyn Singer   John Hendrix

Disney • HYPERION BOOKS
New York

To my zany history-buff brother-in-law, Bob Aronson —M.S.

To Andi Leigh, who loved this book, and me,
from the very beginning —J.H.

ACKNOWLEDGMENTS

Many thanks to Jerry Aronson, Steve Aronson, Brenda Bowen, Andrew Ottiger, Rebecca Dalzell, my wonderful editor, Rotem Moscovich, and Stephanie Lurie and the other fabulous folks at Disney-Hyperion. —M. S.

With gratitude to my magical studio assistant, the talented Audrey Westcott. —J.H.

First Edition
10 9 8 7 6 5 4 3 2 1
F850-6835-5-13196
Printed in Singapore
Library of Congress Cataloging-in-Publication Data
Singer, Marilyn.
[Poems. Selections]
Rutherford B., who was he?: poems about our presidents/Marilyn Singer; John Hendrix.—First edition.
pages cm
ISBN-13: 978-1-4231-7100-3
ISBN-10: 1-4231-7100-4
1. Presidents—United States—Biography—Juvenile poetry. 2. Children's poetry, American. 3. Historical poetry, American.
I. Hendrix, John, 1976- illustrator. II. Title.
PS3569.I546A6 2013 811'.54—dc23 2013010690.
Reinforced binding
Visit www.disneyhyperionbooks.com

Who were these men
who had what it took
to be commander in chief of all the armed forces,
to suggest what to do with our country's resources?

Who were these men?
Not just names in a book:
the ones who stood firm or preferred compromise,
the ones of great stature (though not always size),
the ones we've forgotten, the ones we still prize.

Who were these presidents?
Who were these guys?

ENOUGH TO

MAINTAIN

WHAT I CONSIDER THE MOST ENVIABLE OF ALL...

...TITLES, THE CHARACTER OF AN

HONEST

MAN

GEORGE WASHINGTON
(Independent, 1789–1797)

This great hero of the Revolution,
        after so much strife,
yearned to return to Mount Vernon
        and lead a quiet life.
But the citizens insisted
        his service wasn't done.
They begged him to be president—
        said he was the only one
who could fulfill the mission,
who would invent tradition.

He agreed to father a newborn nation—
and never took a real vacation.

JOHN ADAMS
(Federalist, 1797–1801)

THOMAS JEFFERSON
(Democratic-Republican, 1801–1809)

Adams: We agreed . . .

Jefferson: We agreed . . .

Adams: on that declaration . . .

Jefferson: I composed in the City of Brotherly Love.

Adams: The right to life, liberty, and happiness.

Jefferson: You mean, "the pursuit of."

Adams: And when with my spouse
in the new White House,
I blessed . . .

Jefferson: without a hint of laughter . . .

Adams: . . . all who'd come to live there, after,
that included *you*.

Jefferson: True.
But now you declare the government must be in control.

Adams: And you want the states to rule.
That is your goal!

Jefferson: You shall not hold the people
in your grip!

Adams: Who will end . . .

Jefferson: My former friend . . .

BOTH: . . . this bitter partisanship?

ADAMS
THE MOST VALUABLE of ALL TALENTS IS THAT OF NEVER USING TWO WORDS WHEN ONE WILL DO.

JAMES MADISON

(Democratic-Republican, 1809–1817)

The British were snatching
American sailors
from our merchant ships and whalers.
The Father of the Constitution
tried for peaceful resolution.
But came the year of 1812.
He perceived he had to shelve
his attempts at moderate means
and blow the Royal Navy
to smithereens.
The States were not well prepared.
The citizens were troubled, angry, scared.
Our capital was burned.

But soon the tide roundly turned.
The British quit, for they had learned
America was independent once and for all.
And Madison (just five feet six)
left office ten feet tall.

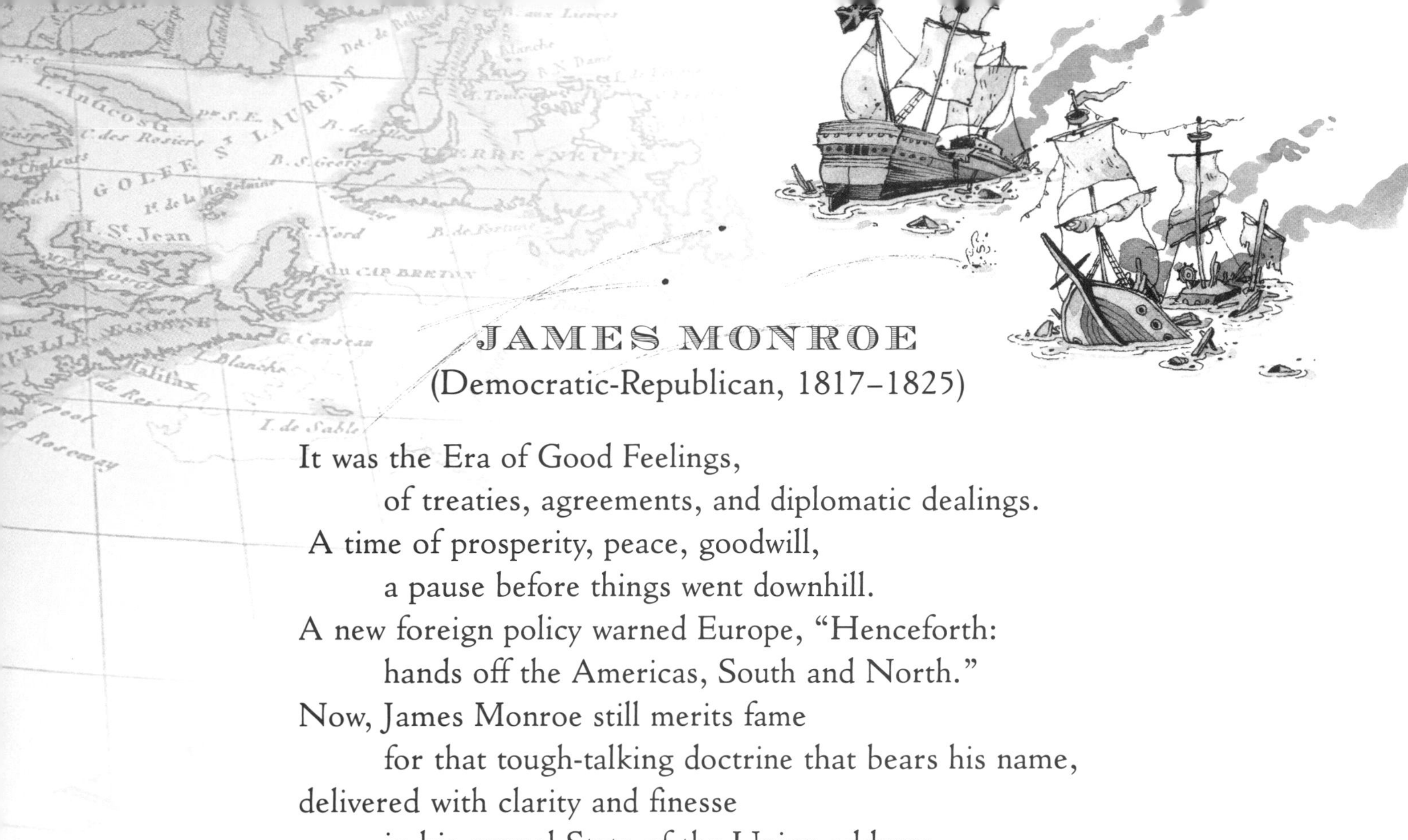

JAMES MONROE

(Democratic-Republican, 1817–1825)

It was the Era of Good Feelings,
of treaties, agreements, and diplomatic dealings.
A time of prosperity, peace, goodwill,
a pause before things went downhill.
A new foreign policy warned Europe, "Henceforth:
hands off the Americas, South and North."
Now, James Monroe still merits fame
for that tough-talking doctrine that bears his name,
delivered with clarity and finesse
in his annual State of the Union address
(though it was written—there is no debate—
by J. Q. Adams, Secretary of State).

IF WE LOOK TO THE HISTORY OF OTHER NATIONS ANCIENT OR MODERN, WE FIND NO EXAMPLE...

...OF A GROWTH SO RAPID, SO GIGANTIC, OF A PEOPLE SO PROSPEROUS AND HAPPY.

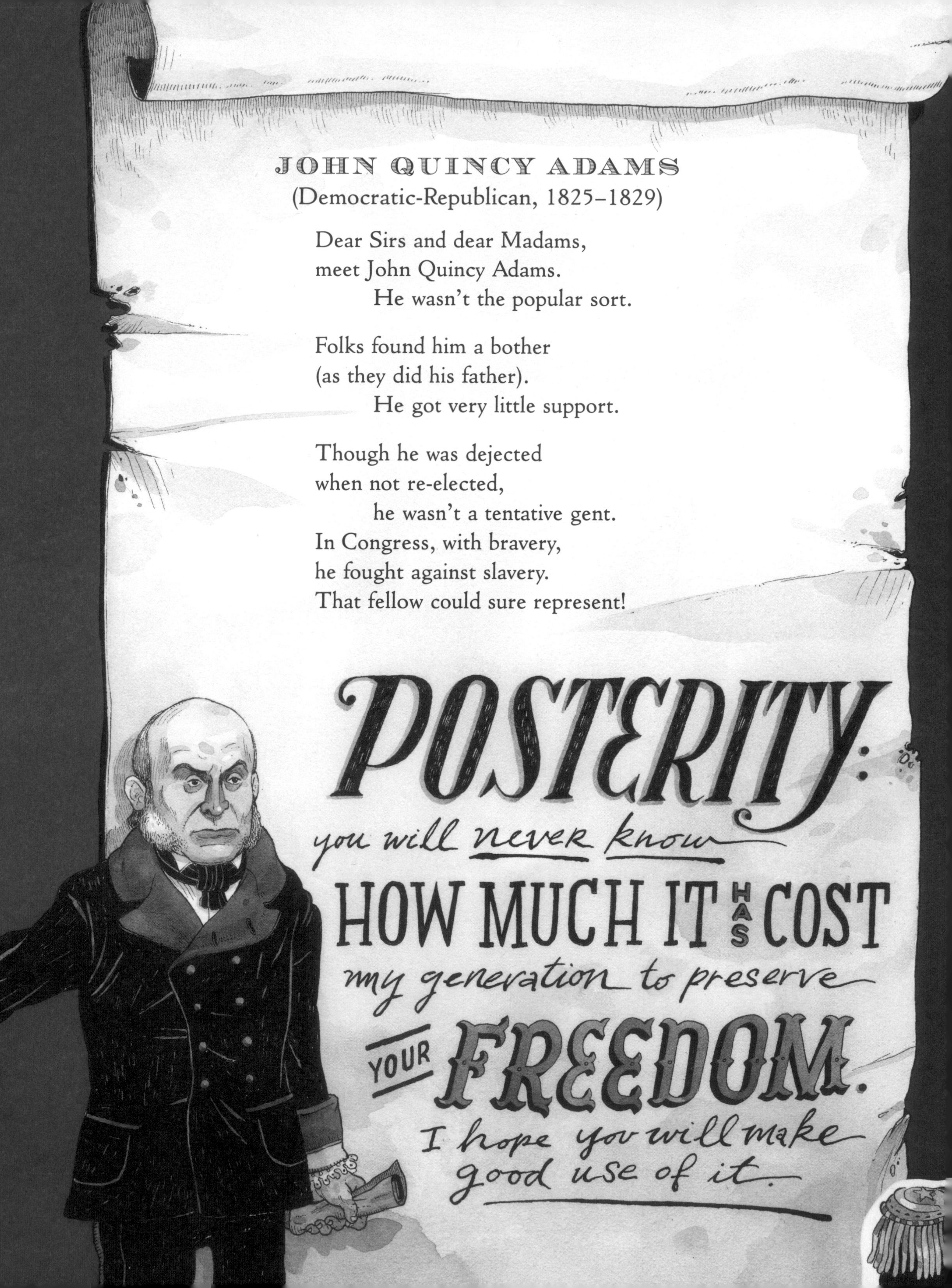

JOHN QUINCY ADAMS
(Democratic-Republican, 1825–1829)

Dear Sirs and dear Madams,
meet John Quincy Adams.
He wasn't the popular sort.

Folks found him a bother
(as they did his father).
He got very little support.

Though he was dejected
when not re-elected,
he wasn't a tentative gent.
In Congress, with bravery,
he fought against slavery.
That fellow could sure represent!

POSTERITY:
you will never know
HOW MUCH IT HAS COST
my generation to preserve
YOUR FREEDOM.
I hope you will make
good use of it.

ANDREW JACKSON
(Democrat, 1829–1837)

MARTIN VAN BUREN
(Democrat, 1837–1841)

We were meant to expand.
It's American to have ambition.

And we deserve the land.

It's our splendid mission
to extend our area of freedom.
The Indians must move farther west.

But what if they refuse?
What if they protest?

We will pay them well.
There, they'll be safe
to govern their own tribes.

What if they won't go for bribes?

Then we'll need to use force.

I see. Of course.

Our great ideals
sometimes lead to strife.
That's why the Cherokee
call me Sharp Knife.

WILLIAM HENRY HARRISON
(Whig, 1841)

Called himself a man of action,
also brainy and well-bred.
Was a general, fought the Shawnee,
studied classics, then pre-med.
At his cold inauguration,
wore no coat—had too much pride.
Gave a long speech, caught pneumonia.
One month later, up and died.

JOHN TYLER

(Whig, 1841–1845)

Singing in praise of Old Tippecanoe,
they always added his name, too.
But he was never meant to be
heir to the throne—His Accidency.
When Congress told him, "We outrank you.
We'll take charge," he said, "No, thank you."
He vetoed their bills. He strongly rebelled.
His party proclaimed, "Why, then—
you're expelled!"
Although those Whigs became his exes,
still he managed to annex Texas.

JAMES K. POLK

(Democrat, 1845–1849)

A dark horse candidate, Jackson's heir,
said, I've got four promises to declare:
I'll lower the tariffs—and quickly, you'll see.
I'll set up a national treasury.
I'll say once and for all, these are Oregon's borders
and give those British their marching orders.
I'll get us California. We won't be polite—
the Mexicans sell, or else we fight!
Once we stretch from coast to coast,
I'll retire and let *you* boast!

A powerful president with lots of gall.
Made four promises, kept them all.

ZACHARY TAYLOR
(Whig, 1849–1850)
MILLARD FILLMORE
(Whig, 1850–1853)
12
13
I swore to preserve the Union.
I roared: Do not secede!
I felt the states should have their rights.
I didn't want this land to bleed.
And so I let the states decide—
Were they slave or were they free?
I'd have hanged those rebels
from the nearest tree.
I said that we should compromise.
No hanging, no graves.
Send back runaway slaves.
I thought I knew the score.
Now, forever unhailed . . .
14
15
I tried . . .
And I failed
to keep us out of civil war.
FRANKLIN PIERCE
(Democrat, 1853–1857)
JAMES BUCHANAN
(Democrat, 1857–1861)

ABRAHAM LINCOLN
(Whig, Republican, 1861–1865)

By stovepipe hat, beard, large size,
    he's the one we recognize.
By addresses of great note,
    he's the one we often quote.
By leading through war—wrenching, bloody—
    he's the one we always study.
By exercising his high station
    to proclaim emancipation,
then meeting such a tragic fate,
    he's the one we rank as great.

ANDREW JOHNSON

(Democrat, 1865–1869)

Let the pardoned South rejoin the Union.
Let the blacks go back to work the fields.
Let Congress know that I am their commander,
    and that a strong commander never yields.
Let them say I cannot oust officials.
I'm not one to do as others bid.
Let Congress bluster that it shall impeach me.
What's that you say—
    Congress *did*?

MY FAILURES HAVE BEEN ERRORS IN JUDGMENT NOT OF INTENT.
GRANT 68
VICKSBURG
SHILOH
GETTYSBURG
WASHINGTON D.C.

ULYSSES S. GRANT
(Republican, 1869–1877)

Leading armies and countries are two different things.
Ask princes and prime ministers. Ask generals and kings.
For heroes are human—they aren't white knights.
In fighting for equality, supporting civil rights,
some succeed skillfully. Others just can't
if they do not like politics and their savvy is scant.

He was loyal to a fault, and also too trusting,
surrounded by scoundrels whose schemes were disgusting.
Though brilliant in battle, he was bound to disenchant
when he became President Ulysses S. Grant.

RUTHERFORD B. HAYES
(Republican, 1877–1881)

Rutherford B., who was he?
Honest and upstanding, or His Fraudulency?
He won a harsh election with disputes and appeals,
(and also quite possibly backroom deals).
He believed in suffrage, thought the South would comply,
that all would get to vote (which proved to be a lie).
He had faith in education and desire for reform,
but he chose to steer a middle path
and not stir up a storm.
He had radical thoughts and conservative ways.
He said so himself, did President Hayes.

JAMES A. GARFIELD

(Republican, 1881)

Anti-unions, anti-greenbacks.
Anti-appointments for party machine hacks
Pro-education and rights for freed blacks.

He won a close election, was eager to begin.
Got shot by a crazed office seeker.
Doctors likely did him in.

CHESTER A. ARTHUR

(Republican, 1881–1885)

To-do list (now that you're president):

Upgrade the navy.
Redo the White House.
    Give those with merit the jobs.
Throw a big party.
Buy yourself new suits.
    (Leaders should never be slobs.)
Reduce the tariffs.
Veto a bad bill.
    (It's wasteful—a barrel of pork.)
You have to take care of the country
    (and not just your friends in New York).

GROVER CLEVELAND

(Democrat, 1885–1889)

He must have struck Congress
as a pesky mosquito,
when over and over
he'd veto and veto
any bill which dared to mention
that Civil War veterans should get a pension.
(Many thought he had some nerve
since he'd chosen not to serve.)
Those soldiers, feeling disrespected,
were glad he wasn't re-elected.

BENJAMIN HARRISON

(Republican, 1889–1893)

This Civil War vet signed a bill with one stroke,
paying millions in pensions.
The country went broke.
(He also raised tariffs,
depleted our gold,
and even his aides found his manner quite cold.)
The commander in chief took so much flak,
the voters brought the last guy back.

GROVER CLEVELAND

(Democrat, 1893–1897)

"We will return," said Cleveland's spouse
the day they left their stately house.
She was right—the chief executive
had four more years (though nonconsecutive).
Although he tried to quell unrest,
America remained depressed.
An honest man of firm decision,
he never had far-reaching vision.
The U.S. would wait a few years longer
for a leader who was stronger.

WHEN YOU PLAY
PLAY·HARD
WHEN·YOU·WORK, ·DON'T·PLAY·AT·ALL.

WILLIAM MCKINLEY

(Republican, 1897–1901)

He knew about battlefields;
he knew about pain.
He was not in a hurry
to clash with Spain.
But when the press cried,
"Remember the *Maine*!"
for the ship that exploded near Cuba's shore,
he was swiftly forced to endorse a war.

The fight was never evenhanded—
America won and then expanded:
the Philippines, Cuba, Puerto Rico, Guam
all fell into our country's palm.
Basking in imperial glory, he added Hawaii
(but that's another story).

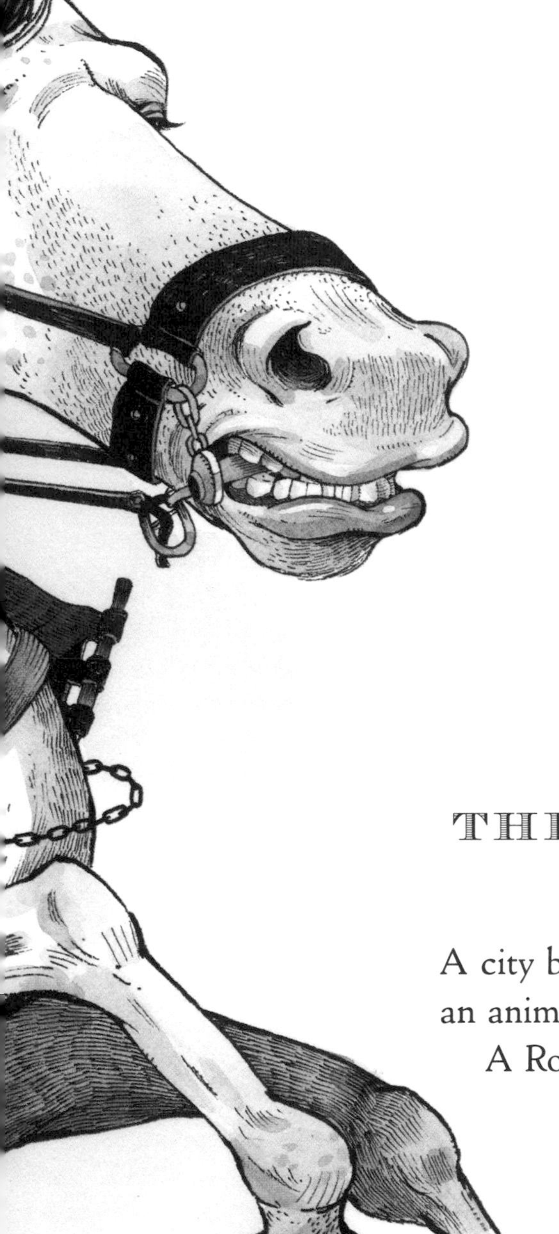

THEODORE ROOSEVELT

(Republican, 1901–1909)

A city boy, who loved the country,
an animal lover, who loved to hunt.
A Rough Rider, rancher, and a scholar,
a diplomat, yet also blunt.
He took on greedy corporations
and foreign powers with this trick:
A president should speak quite softly,
but always carry a very large stick.

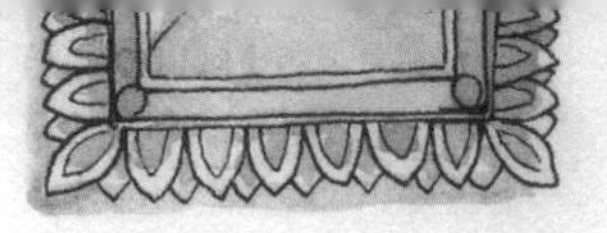

WILLIAM HOWARD TAFT

(Republican, 1909–1913)

Theodore Roosevelt had to give him the nudge:
Taft became president. But he was a drudge.
Poor man, so unhappy, became such a pudge.
Got stuck in the bathtub and just couldn't budge.
Was pleased to leave office and instead be a judge.

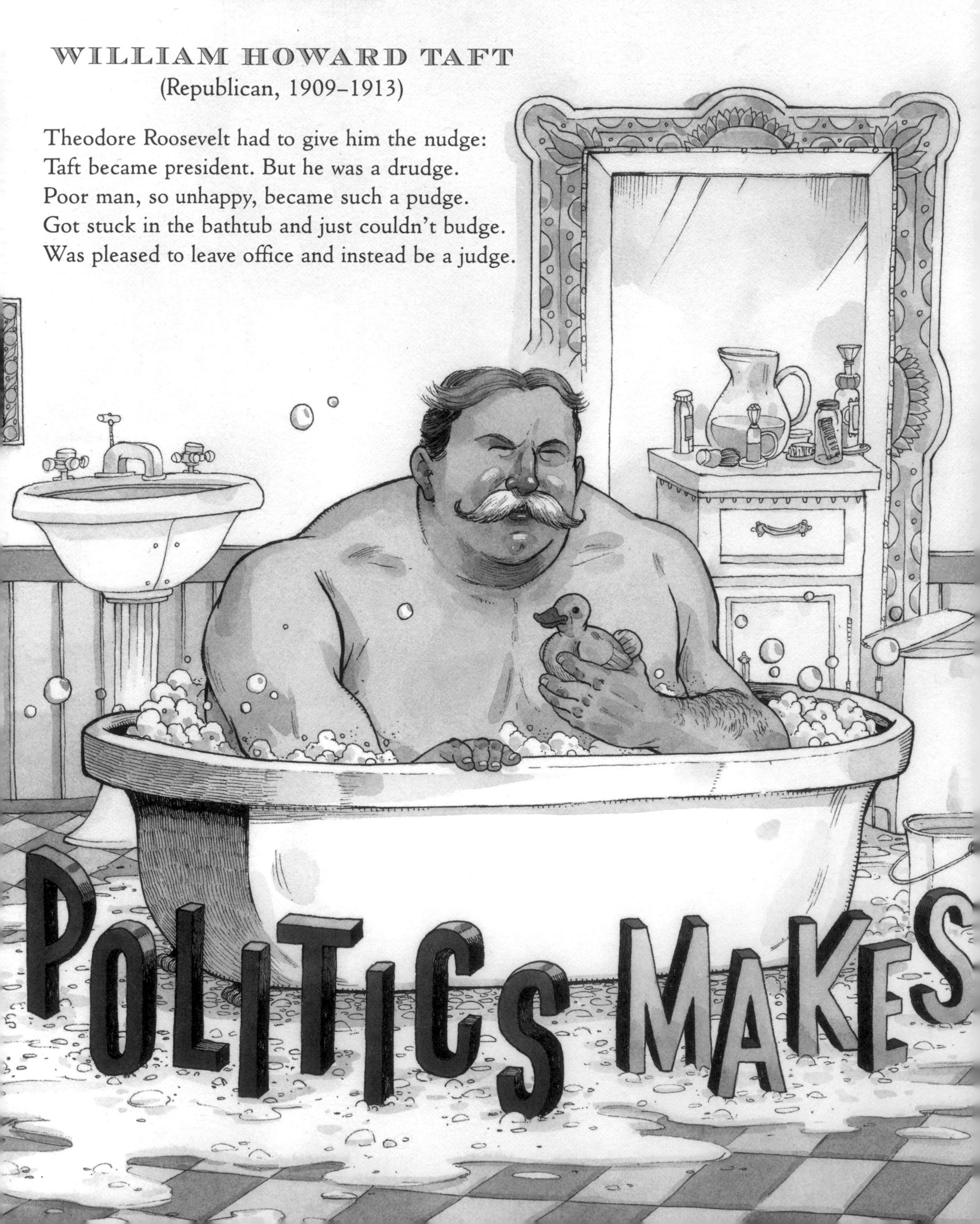

WOODROW WILSON

(Democrat, 1913–1921)

The most peace-loving leaders give up their credos
    when faced with attacks from German torpedoes.
So Wilson declared we must take up the gun
    and side with the Allies in World War I.
When it was over, he called for a league
    of nations to bring to light foreign intrigue,
coming together for session after session
    to settle disputes and prevent armed aggression.
The most determined leaders, no matter how skilled,
    don't always live to see their dreams fulfilled.
The U.S. wouldn't join. It was left to other men
    thirty years later to establish the U.N.

WARREN G. HARDING
(Republican, 1921–1923)

Charming, good-looking, and touchy-feely.
Did he want to be president? No, not really.
His ambitious missus was said to gloat
that she'd gotten him the women's vote.
The job was more than he could handle.
There'd soon be scandal after scandal.
He decided to take a cross-country tour.
He'd meet the public. He was sure
they'd be open, understanding.
They'd like his speeches and glad-handing.
With his health, it was a risk, though.
His heart gave out in San Francisco.

CALVIN COOLIDGE

(Republican, 1923–1929)

Speculation! People scrambling
to invest—a kind of gambling.
It was easy to get credit—spending soared.
They called him Silent Cal,
while the twenties roared.

More autos on the highways.
More airplanes on the flyways.
With radio and movies, who was bored?
They kept cool with Mr. Coolidge,
while the twenties roared.

Though there was Prohibition,
people had less inhibition
at speakeasies, where the drinks and music poured.
Lots of fun, lots of cash
(till the Stock Market Crash).
Calvin Coolidge stayed at home and snored.
They say he left the White House still adored
while the Roaring Twenties . . . roared.

ANYONE
HERBERT · HOOVER
BUT HIM
I ASK YOU TO JUDGE ME
CBS

HERBERT HOOVER
(Republican, 1929–1933)

A chicken in every pot, two cars in every garage.
Millionaire and business whiz—
folks sneered that every pot was *his*.
He wasn't uncaring, yet held the strong belief
that government should not provide financial relief.
The Great Depression—not his fault. But he got the blame.
In the thirties Herbert Hoover was a dirty name.
Up for re-election, he knew his chance was grim
when the public's slogan was ANYONE BUT HIM.

FRANKLIN D. ROOSEVELT
(Democrat, 1933–1945)

Four terms (almost) to cope
with the Great Depression,
to offer a New Deal,
to battle aggression
in Europe and the South Pacific
(World War II, to be specific).

Four terms (almost) to leave
quite an impression,
to lead year after year
when there was more than just fear

to *fear*.

HARRY S. TRUMAN

(Democrat, 1945–1953)

No one was brasher
than that former haberdasher,
more prone to fury
than that man from Missouri,
who rose from running a clothing store
to overseeing the end of a war—
then started a new one
(an out-of-the-blue one).
Some said he did too little.
Some said he did too much.
That, yes, he was on top of things!
No, he was out of touch!
One thing is certain—
he made it quite clear.
The burden was his:
THE BUCK STOPS HERE.

DWIGHT D. EISENHOWER
(Republican, 1953–1961)

They liked Ike.
He was a closer.
They liked Ike.
He wasn't a poser.

He planned the D-day invasions,
ended war with Korea.
He pushed for interstate highways—
an enterprising idea.

Ike liked golf
and quiet command.
Ike liked governing
with a "hidden hand."

He said the U.S. should wage peace,
while flaunting nuclear power.
He took no credit, took no heat—
Dwight D. Eisenhower.

JOHN F. KENNEDY

(Democrat, 1961–1963)

Vision and television made him a star.
He told us we would travel far
in the Peace Corps, to outer space.
But there were perils we would face:
Soviet missiles at our back door,
the alarming threat of nuclear war,
the growing strife in Vietnam.
His was not a time of calm.
Yet he gave us hope. He gave us the Moon.
He gave us a presidency that ended too soon.

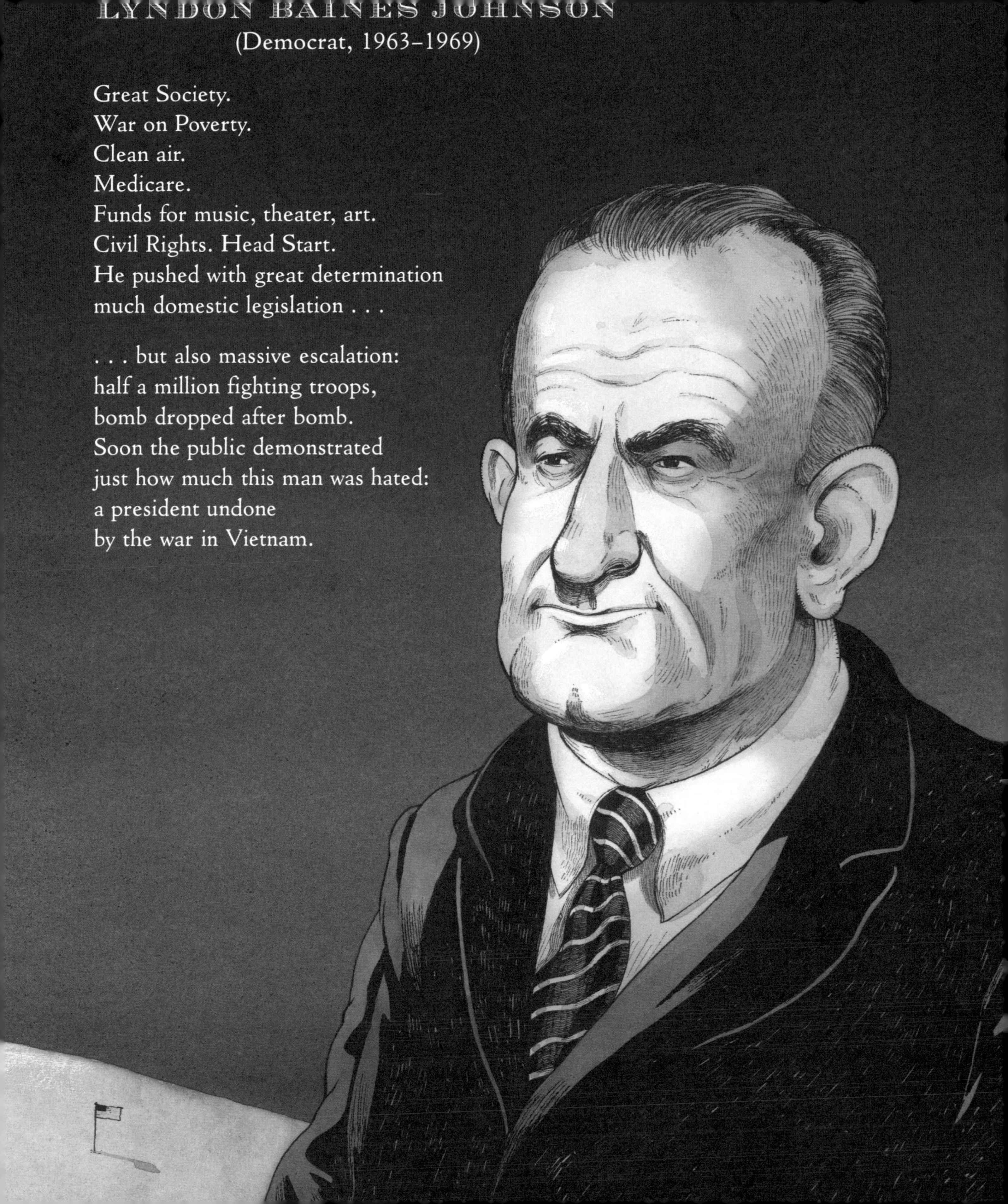

LYNDON BAINES JOHNSON

(Democrat, 1963–1969)

Great Society.
War on Poverty.
Clean air.
Medicare.
Funds for music, theater, art.
Civil Rights. Head Start.
He pushed with great determination
much domestic legislation . . .

. . . but also massive escalation:
half a million fighting troops,
bomb dropped after bomb.
Soon the public demonstrated
just how much this man was hated:
a president undone
by the war in Vietnam.

RICHARD NIXON

(Republican, 1969–1974)

Forced to resign
with a tarnished reputation,
as the president
known
to be
tricky,
he must have mourned his lost accomplishments.
Who protected the environment?
Who opened the gateway to China?
Would people remember
Watergate, nothing but Watergate?

Watergate, nothing but Watergate.
Would people remember
who opened the gateway to China,
who protected the environment?
He must have mourned his lost accomplishments.
Tricky
to be
known
as the president
with a tarnished reputation,
forced to resign.

GERALD R. FORD

(Republican, 1974–1977)

Selected, not elected.
Few had taken note of him.
None cast a single vote for him
as president or veep.
When both resigned, he made the leap.
Welcomed at first, his bubble soon burst.
He got in a fix when
he pardoned Dick Nixon.
He thought he was healing a troubled nation.
Instead, he damaged his own reputation.
Congress refused cooperation.
By the time his honor was fully restored,
he was no longer President Gerald R. Ford.

JIMMY CARTER

(Democrat, 1977–1981)

An unknown politician,
a Georgia peanut farmer,
he wore his forthright style
like a suit of armor.

He pledged to clean up government.
Folks took to this newcomer.
But soon his ratings slipped
one aggravating summer:

Autos lined up at the pumps.
Rising crude oil prices.
Then suddenly, on top of that,
the Iran hostage crisis.

He didn't win a second term,
but earned a Nobel Prize
for his work in human rights.
His rank began to rise.

Some presidents while serving
are often underrated.
As an elder statesman, this one's
highly celebrated.

RONALD REAGAN

(Republican, 1981–1989)

REPUBLICANS: Such a great hero! His words still inspire!
He challenged, then brought down an evil empire!
He knew how to make the economy boom
(and also how to work a room).
We think he should be on Mount Rushmore. . . .

DEMOCRATS: Good grief, could the GOP gush more?
His budget and tax cuts helped to insure
the rich would get richer, the poor stay poor.
A salesman, an actor, who helped us get
deeper and deeper into debt.
Not someone we should idolize. . . .

HISTORIANS: How to view him? Through whose eyes?
When it comes to presidents, both foe and fan
find it hard to separate the myth from the man.

GEORGE H. W. BUSH

(Republican, 1989–1993)

He had much experience in foreign affairs,
didn't let crises take him unawares.
He was able to deal with Kuwait and Iraq
and the collapse of the Soviet Bloc.
He was calm, he was cool, he had been the V.P.
He gave all the voters a guarantee:
he wouldn't raise taxes; he'd balance the budget.
But he couldn't oblige. There was no way to fudge it.
He hoped to serve longer. He did not want to quit.
But Bush lost his job to the deficit.

BILL CLINTON
(Democrat, 1993–2001)

He was Arkansas's governor, a hip jazz cat.
He labeled himself a "New Democrat."
There was trouble with the budget—he thought a lot
about where he could cut it and where he would not.
He disagreed with Congress and vowed to hang tough.
Said, "You're planning to shut down? I'm calling your bluff!"
The economy flourished. It seemed like win-win.
Then came the scandals, the trial, the chagrin.
Might there have been heights that he could have reached
had he not been distracted, not been impeached?

GEORGE W. BUSH

(Republican, 2001–2009)

A contested win—
 two parties polarized.
A nightmarish attack—
 a country traumatized.
Plans that he intended—
 suddenly upended,
 overridden by the War on Terror.
Was the strategy right,
 was it in error?
Perhaps he's correct—
 only history will tell.
What's certain is his whole world changed,
 the day the towers fell.

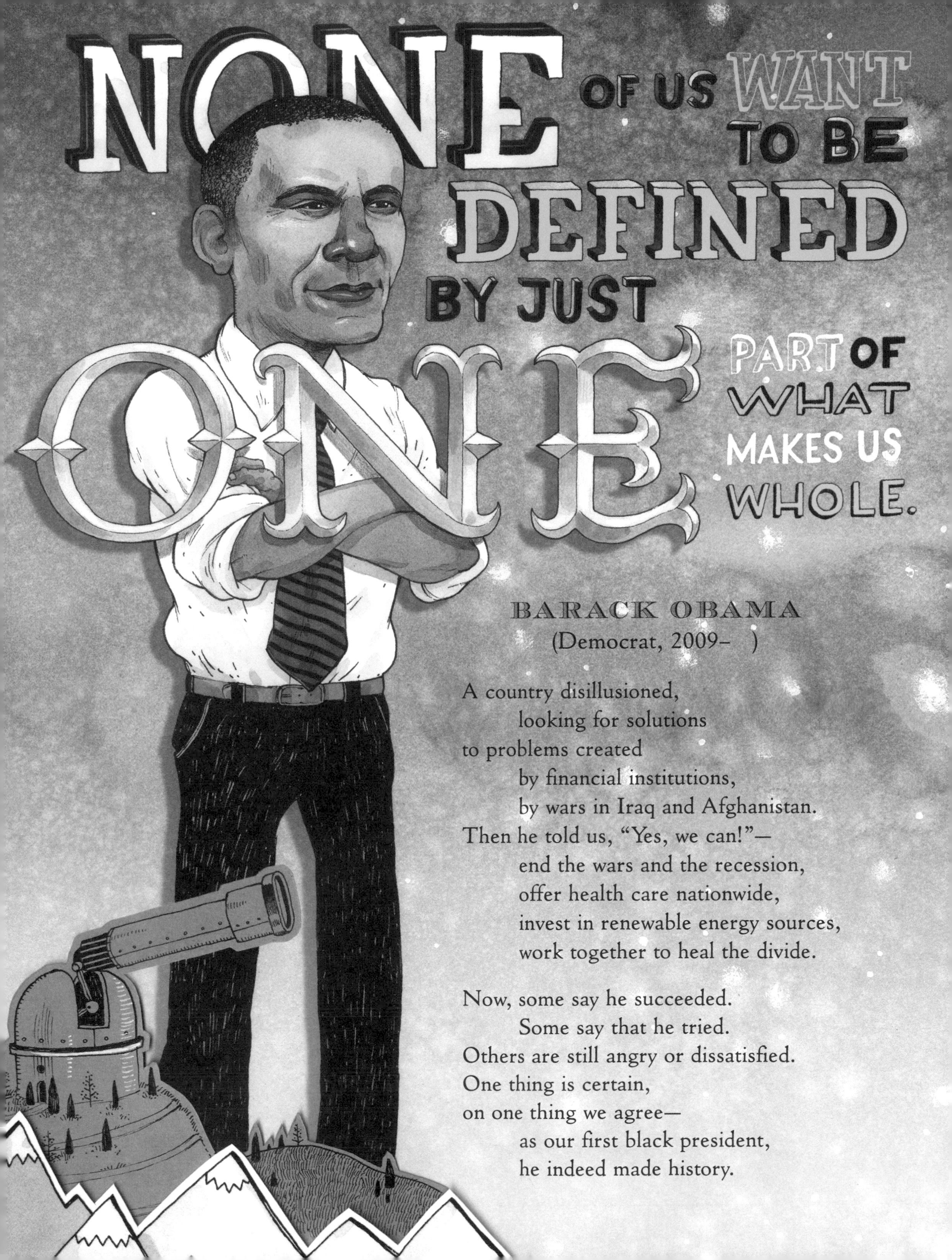

BARACK OBAMA
(Democrat, 2009–)

A country disillusioned,
looking for solutions
to problems created
by financial institutions,
by wars in Iraq and Afghanistan.
Then he told us, "Yes, we can!"—
end the wars and the recession,
offer health care nationwide,
invest in renewable energy sources,
work together to heal the divide.

Now, some say he succeeded.
Some say that he tried.
Others are still angry or dissatisfied.
One thing is certain,
on one thing we agree—
as our first black president,
he indeed made history.

MEET THE PRESIDENT

Chief executive. Head of state. Commander in chief. POTUS. Those are all names for the president of the United States. To become president, a person must be at least thirty-five years old, American-born, and a resident of this country for a minimum of fourteen years. And then, of course, he or she must be elected.

Once elected, the president becomes the head of the executive branch of government. He or she is now the commander in chief of the armed forces and can negotiate treaties with other countries, nominate ambassadors, and set foreign policy. The president can propose new laws, but cannot pass them. That's the job of the legislative branch—Congress. Once Congress passes a law, the president can sign it into law or veto it. He or she can also present a budget to Congress (and Congress can offer changes to that budget). Though the president takes an oath to "preserve, protect, and defend the Constitution of the United States," he or she cannot decide what is or isn't constitutional. That's up to the judicial branch—namely the Supreme Court. The president appoints the justices to this court, but they must be approved by Congress.

Over the years, some presidents have been stronger leaders than others. However, the office of the president has grown larger and more powerful. Today, the president is involved in a wide range of domestic and global issues. He—and perhaps, in the future, she—is a leader whose face and name are known throughout the world.

PRESIDENTIAL BIOGRAPHIES

GEORGE WASHINGTON is the only chief executive who was not a member of a political party and who was unanimously chosen by the electoral college to be president of the United States—a job he didn't really want. But by accepting it, he held together a struggling new nation. He was the first to carry out the constitutional principle that the federal government was the supreme law of the land, with the right to collect taxes and to call out a militia to end invasion or rebellion. Though he strongly disliked partisanship, he could not prevent two opposing parties from forming: the Democratic-Republicans, led by Thomas Jefferson, and the Federalists, headed by Alexander Hamilton. Critics point to his inability to establish a plan for the abolition of slavery as one of the failures of his administration. In general, historians agree that his achievements were great and lasting, and that he truly deserves the title "Father of Our Country."

"I hope I shall possess firmness and virtue enough to maintain what I consider the most enviable of all titles, the character of an honest man." —G.W.

America's first vice president and second president, **JOHN ADAMS** was a passionate patriot known to be brilliant, stubborn, and prickly. His was the first family to live in the White House. Adams's term in office was troubled by crises in foreign policy, particularly with France. A Federalist who believed in a strong central government, Adams often clashed with his vice president and colleague, Thomas Jefferson, a Democratic-Republican who favored limited federal power. The two eventually reunited when both were out of office. Adams's last words were "Jefferson still lives." He didn't realize that his friend and rival had died a few hours before—on July 4, 1826.

"I pray Heaven to bestow the best of blessings on this house and all that shall hereafter inhabit it. May none but honest and wise men ever rule under this roof."—J.A.

Farmer, architect, inventor, and author of the Declaration of Independence, **THOMAS JEFFERSON** won a difficult election against John Adams to become third president of the United States. His election laid the groundwork for the two-party system. Like Adams, during his presidency he faced battles between the two political parties, many centering on the judicial branch. The result was that the independent power of the Supreme Court was established. Jefferson was responsible for the Louisiana Purchase, which doubled the size of the U.S. Though he wrote that all men are created equal, Jefferson was himself a slaveholder who never emancipated his slaves. This contradiction set the stage for many more serious conflicts to come in both presidential and American history.

"The most valuable of all talents is that of never using two words when one will do." —T.J.

Originally a Federalist, **JAMES MADISON**, chief author of the Constitution, formed the Democratic-Republican Party along with Thomas Jefferson. As Jefferson's secretary of state and then as president, Madison attempted to solve issues with Great Britain through peaceful means. But the problems continued, particularly impressment—British ships seizing American sailors to serve in the Royal Navy—and in 1812, Madison was pressured to declare war. For a time, things went poorly for America. The British marched on Washington, D.C., and burned buildings, including the Capitol and the White House. But shortly thereafter, key U.S. victories boosted morale, and Americans who had opposed the war and disliked Madison found new respect for their president.

"The happy Union of these States is a wonder; their Constitution a miracle; their example the hope of Liberty throughout the world." —J.M.

At the start of **JAMES MONROE**'s presidency, Americans were celebrating the "Era of Good Feelings"—victory in the War of 1812, financial prosperity, and less partisanship. But soon Monroe, the last Federalist president, faced several crises, including an economic depression and the entrance to the Union of Missouri as a slave state. He supported the Missouri Compromise, which prohibited slavery in states acquired in the Louisiana Purchase north of the 36°30' latitude. The policy for which he remains most famous is the "Monroe Doctrine," which was actually written by John Quincy Adams. It stated that any attempts by European countries to interfere with areas or countries in North or South America would be viewed as acts of aggression. To this day, debates rage over this doctrine—has it discouraged colonialism or encouraged American imperialism?

"If we look to the history of other nations, ancient or modern, we find no example of a growth so rapid, so gigantic, of a people so prosperous and happy."—J.M.

The son of John Adams, **JOHN QUINCY ADAMS** was an effective secretary of state and an ineffective president. Adams's own party did not support him and blocked his initiatives, which included national construction of roads, canals, and bridges. After serving four years as president, Adams was elected to the House of Representatives, where he served brilliantly for nine terms. An ardent abolitionist, he won freedom for the slaves who mutinied on the Spanish ship *Amistad*. His talent as a forceful, articulate congressional speaker earned him the nickname "Old Man Eloquent" and lasting historical acclaim.

"Posterity: you will never know how much it has cost my generation to preserve your freedom. I hope you will make good use of it."—J.Q.A.

ANDREW JACKSON has been viewed as both a man of the people and a tyrant. He supported giving *all* white males the right to vote—not just landowners. He established the "spoils system"—handing out jobs as rewards to his supporters. Jackson and his followers, the Democrats who split off from the Democratic-Republican Party, felt that the government should have limited power and that concentrated wealth was a danger to liberty, so he refused to renew the charter of the Bank of the United States. Defying Congress, he removed its funds and placed them in state banks, which mismanaged the money, resulting in a financial depression shortly after he left office. Though there is evidence that he did not personally hate Native Americans, Jackson wanted their lands and felt that he knew what was best for them. He pushed for the Indian Removal Act, the only major law that Congress passed at Jackson's bidding during his two terms in office. It led to one of the saddest chapters in American history.

"I was born for the storm, and a calm does not suit me."—A.J.

The Indian Removal Act claimed that Native Americans were asked to move voluntarily in exchange for money and new land west of the Mississippi. Some Indian nations signed treaties with the government, but others refused. Jackson's successor, **MARTIN VAN BUREN**, supported forced removal of the Cherokee people. The march to Indian Territory in what is now eastern Oklahoma, during which one quarter of the Cherokee nation died of disease, famine, or exposure, is known as the Trail of Tears. Van Buren had united the Democratic Party behind Jackson and won his own election by promising to carry on Jackson's policies, but he didn't expect to inherit a financial depression. His failure to fix the economy cost him a second term in office.

"I tread in the footsteps of illustrious men . . . in receiving from the people the sacred trust confided to my illustrious predecessor."—M.V.B.

WILLIAM HENRY HARRISON came from an aristocratic, slaveholding family. He went to college, then left to study premedicine under an eminent physician. Nevertheless, he ran for president as a humble frontiersman and as a war hero in both the Battle of Tippecanoe against the Shawnee in 1811, and during the war of 1812. Elected president at the age of 68, Harrison wanted to show the public that he was still fit, so on a cold and wet March day, he stood without a coat or hat and spoke for two hours—the longest inaugural speech in American history. He caught pneumonia and died one month later—the shortest term for any U.S. president.

"The American backwoodsman—clad in his hunting shirt, the product of this domestic industry, and fighting for the country he loves, he is more than a match for the vile but splendid mercenary of a European despot."—W.H.H.

"Tippecanoe and Tyler, too," was the campaign slogan of William Henry Harrison and his running mate, **JOHN TYLER**. Both Harrison and Tyler were members of the Whig party, which had broken off from the Democratic-Republicans in disagreement with Andrew Jackson's policies. When Harrison died, there was confusion about whether Tyler would be an acting or an actual president. The Whigs, who were in the majority in both the cabinet and legislative branch, claimed that Congress was in charge. Tyler firmly disagreed and had himself sworn in as president, earning him the nickname "His Accidency." When Tyler vetoed a bill to reestablish the national bank—an institution that the Whigs favored—his cabinet resigned. Later, the Whigs expelled him from their party. Still, he managed to get Congress to pass a joint resolution to annex Texas. It was admitted as a slave state, which further increased tensions between pro- and anti-slavery forces and helped set the stage for the Civil War.

"I can never consent to being dictated to."—J.T.

"Who is **JAMES K. POLK**?"mocked his Whig opponents during his campaign. Few people had ever heard of the candidate, whose platform consisted of four major goals, all of which he fulfilled: 1) to lower the tariffs on imports to promote free trade; 2) to stabilize the banking system by creating a national treasury; 3) to settle the borders of the Oregon Territory; and 4) to acquire California and claim disputed territory in Texas. There was a conflict between the U.S. and Great Britain over the borders of the Oregon Territory (which included what is now Oregon, Idaho, and Washington states). Polk's famous campaign slogan "Fifty-four Forty or Fight!" referred to the latitude of the border that Americans wanted. He compromised with the British and set the American border at the forty-ninth parallel. The Mexicans were willing neither to compromise on the Texas borders nor to sell California (which included what is now New Mexico), so Polk waged war, eventually acquiring these areas. By the time he left office, he had managed to add more than one million square miles to the United States. What Polk didn't resolve during his term was the question of whether these new territories would be open to slavery or be free states. And that was the major question that haunted his successors.

"In truth, though I occupy a very high position, I am the hardest-working man in this country."—J.K.P.

A hero of the Mexican War, **ZACHARY TAYLOR**—Old Rough and Ready—was a wealthy slave owner who wanted the new territories acquired from Mexico to decide for themselves whether to join the Union as free or slave states, all the while knowing they would choose the former. He believed in a strong union and threatened to hang secessionists, including his daughter's husband, Jefferson Davis, who went on to become president of the Confederacy. Taylor's presidency was short-lived; he died after a year in office, most likely of cholera.

"For more than half a century, during which kingdoms and empires have fallen, this Union has stood unshaken. The patriots who formed it have long since descended to the grave; yet still it remains, the proudest monument to their memory. . . . In my judgment, its dissolution would be the greatest of calamities."—Z.T.

Hoping to safeguard the Union, **MILLARD FILLMORE**, the last Whig president, signed the Compromise of 1850, which his predecessor had opposed. Among its clauses, this compromise included the Fugitive Slave Act, which required all citizens to assist in the return of runaway slaves. Although the compromise may have temporarily kept the country out of war, this act and other parts of the compromise further embittered relations between North and South.

"An honorable defeat is better than a dishonorable victory."—M.F.

A Northerner, **FRANKLIN PIERCE** opposed the abolition of slavery in the South. He also believed that the Missouri Compromise of 1820, which banned slavery in various territories, would be declared unconstitutional by the Supreme Court. But a group of senators did not want to wait for that to happen, so they pressured him into signing the Kansas-Nebraska Act, allowing the territories to decide for themselves whether to be slave or free ("popular sovereignty"). The clash between pro- and anti-slavery sides resulted in "Bleeding Kansas," and the violence tore the state and country apart.

"With the Union my best and dearest earthly hopes are entwined."—F.P.

Many hoped that **JAMES BUCHANAN** would be able to avert Civil War. Another Northerner who believed in popular sovereignty, Buchanan was sympathetic to the South. He endorsed a pro-slavery constitution for the state of Kansas. When fellow Democrats challenged the endorsement, the party split—allowing Republican Abraham Lincoln to win the next election. Six weeks before Lincoln took office, South Carolina seceded from the Union. Buchanan did nothing to stop the secession. When he left the White House, Buchanan, like his predecessor Pierce, retreated to his home and vanished from public life.

"Our union rests upon public opinion, and can never be cemented by the blood of its citizens shed in civil war."—J.B.

A gifted speaker with a memorable appearance, **ABRAHAM LINCOLN** presided over perhaps the most painful period in American history: the Civil War, during which well over half a million Americans died. Though Lincoln was opposed to slavery, he went to war initially to preserve the union. But once the conflict started, he was called upon by free blacks and abolitionists to issue the Emancipation Proclamation, which made ending slavery a goal of the war. Five days after the South surrendered, Lincoln was assassinated at Ford's Theatre in Washington, D.C., by John Wilkes Booth, a supporter of the Confederacy. After his death—or because of it—Lincoln became an almost-mythological hero. In truth, he was a human being—albeit an exceptional one.

"I am a slow walker, but I never walk back."—A.L.

ANDREW JOHNSON was also the target of the Lincoln assassination plot, but his would-be assassin did not go through with the plan. Though Johnson disagreed with secession, he was in favor of slavery. While Congress was in recess, he tried by himself to carry out post–Civil War Reconstruction efforts. He pardoned many in the South and refused to give any rights to freed slaves. When Congress returned, he vetoed bills that granted these rights. Congress overrode his vetoes and eventually passed the Fourteenth Amendment, which declared that all people born or naturalized in the U.S. are citizens with the right to equal protection under the law. When Congress passed a law forbidding the president to remove certain federal officials without the Senate's approval, Johnson struck back by replacing the secretary of war. That was the last straw—Congress impeached him. They failed to remove him from office by one vote. But for the rest of his term, Johnson was a tamed president.

"If I am shot at, I want no man to be in the way of the bullet."—A.J.

A famed general who led the Union troops to victory in the Civil War, **ULYSSES S. GRANT** was not able to lead the country effectively as president. An honorable man himself, he was not a good judge of character. He appointed men who were implicated in corrupt schemes: one involved railroad companies overcharging millions of dollars for government contracts. Believing in suffrage for all American men, Grant tried to use both legal and military protection for freed slaves. Eventually, because of the cost and the decline of public interest in the Reconstruction, Grant could no longer offer these protections. In his farewell address to Congress, he apologized for his errors in judgment and said it had been his "misfortune to be called to the Office of Chief Executive without any political training."

"My failures have been errors in judgment, not of intent."—U.S.G.

RUTHERFORD B. HAYES ran against Samuel Tilden in a bitterly contested election. An Electoral Commission consisting of seven Republicans, seven Democrats, and one Independent was supposed to issue a fair ruling of the disputed votes. But an attempt by Tilden's nephew to influence the Independent led to his replacement by a Republican. That tipped the balance, and Hayes won. Some called it fraud. A reformer, Hayes was against the spoils system, and he believed that education was the best way to equalize society, although he felt that changes had to be made slowly, not swiftly. Like Grant, Hayes supported military-protected suffrage for all men. However, by the time he took office, Reconstruction had all but ended. Hayes pledged to remove the last remaining troops if the South promised to uphold universal voting rights. He kept his word. The South did not.

"I am a radical in thought (and principle) and a conservative in method (and conduct)."—R.B.H.

An eight-term congressman, **JAMES GARFIELD** was pro-abolition and pro-civil rights. He believed in the gold standard—that "greenbacks," the first paper money ever issued by the U.S., had to be backed up by gold in the treasury. Garfield opposed labor unions and felt that the federal government should be allowed to break up strikes. When he became president, he was besieged by people seeking government jobs, which convinced him of the need for civil service reform. One of the office-seekers was a mentally disturbed man named Charles Guiteau. When Garfield refused to appoint him as a consul, Guiteau shot the president at a train station in Washington, D.C. Many feel that his doctors, who did not know about sterilization, caused the president's death when they attempted to remove the bullet. Garfield lingered for over two months before dying of complications from blood poisoning.

"A brave man is a man who dares to look the Devil in the face and tell him he is a Devil."—J.G.

Before he became vice president, **CHESTER A. ARTHUR** was Collector for the Port of New York, a prized post given to him by Roscoe Conkling, a U.S. senator and Republican party boss who often handed out jobs as rewards to his supporters. James Garfield had reluctantly accepted Arthur as his running mate because he knew he needed New York votes. When Garfield was assassinated, Arthur became president, and he proved to be something of a surprise. Instead of being a political puppet, he continued Garfield's reform policies, which included vetoing pork barrel bills—bills that sponsored local projects to get votes from those districts—and supporting the Pendleton Act, which required civil service exams for job seekers. A fashionable man who redecorated the White House and threw lavish parties there, he earned the nickname "The Gentleman Boss."

"Since I came here I have learned that Chester A. Arthur is one man and the President of the United States is another."—C.A.A.

GROVER CLEVELAND was the only chief executive to serve two *nonconsecutive* terms, making him both the twenty-second and the twenty-fourth president. He saw himself as a reformer, but he did not believe that the president should propose new legislation. However, he firmly believed in vetoing bills that he felt were wasteful. In his first term, he set a record by vetoing 413 of them, hundreds of which involved private pensions, particularly for Civil War veterans. When he ran for a second term, the pension issue was likely a factor in his loss.

"Though the people support the government, the government should not support the people."—G.C.

The grandson of short-lived president William Henry Harrison, **BENJAMIN HARRISON** had been a Union general during the Civil War. Nicknamed "the human iceberg" for his frosty manner, he lost the popular vote to Cleveland, but won the electoral college vote. As president, he quickly signed a bill granting generous pensions, which had the effect of seriously draining federal funds. He approved the Sherman Silver Purchase Act, requiring that silver be used for coins. The act also specified that the government would pay for the silver supplies with bank notes that could be exchanged for either silver or gold. The suppliers went for the gold, depleting its supply. These policies resulted in the Depression of 1893—and the re-election of Grover Cleveland.

"I knew that my staying up would not change the election result if I were defeated, while if elected I had a hard day ahead of me. So I thought a night's rest was best in any event."—B.H.

GROVER CLEVELAND did not have a successful second term. He was unable to ease the depression. Labor, hurt by wage cuts, began to unionize. In perhaps the most famous incident from that period, workers for the Pullman railroad car company, joined by other members of the American Railway Union led by Eugene V. Debs, walked off the job. Cleveland called in 12,000 army troops to end the strike. Thirteen workers died and many others were wounded. Six days after the strike ended, Cleveland and Congress attempted to make amends with workers by creating a holiday to honor their efforts. We celebrate it today with parades and picnics: Labor Day.

"A truly American sentiment recognizes the dignity of labor and the fact that honor lies in honest toil."—G.C.

WILLIAM MCKINLEY survived the Civil War, and he knew full well the cost of combat. So he wanted to deal peacefully with Cuba's struggle for independence from Spain—a conflict that was hurting American business. When a small riot erupted in Havana, he sent in the U.S.S. *Maine* to protect American citizens and property there. The ship exploded, most likely because of an internal fire that ignited the gunpowder supply. But the press blamed Spain and trumpeted the slogan, "Remember the *Maine*!" McKinley had to declare war. When America won, Spain was forced to give up its colonies: the Philippines, Puerto Rico, and Guam. The U.S. also got control of Cuba and established a permanent military base there: Guantanamo Bay. America had become a major colonial power. McKinley added to the expansion by annexing Hawaii. In 1901, McKinley was shot by anarchist Leon Czolgosz. His assassination led to charging the Secret Service with the protection of leaders and candidates for office.

"That's all a man can hope for during his lifetime—to set an example—and when he is dead, to be an inspiration for history."—W.M.

A sickly boy, **THEODORE ROOSEVELT** grew up to be an athlete and a rugged individualist. He loved to hunt, was a rancher and sheriff out west, and led the Rough Riders in the Spanish-American War. He was also a scholar who went to Harvard, wrote numerous books, and scuffled with his own Republican party in New York when he became that state's governor. As the vice president, he succeeded McKinley when the president was assassinated. A believer in progressive policies, Roosevelt created the "Square Deal," which included welfare legislation, government regulation of industry, and other reforms. As an environmentalist, he set aside nearly 200 million acres as national forests and preserves. With the approach "Speak softly and carry a big stick," he worked to make America a global power. One of his greatest achievements was the building of the Panama Canal. An immensely popular chief executive, Roosevelt made that office, rather than Congress or political parties, the center of American politics.

"When you play, play hard. When you work, don't play at all."—T.R.

Theodore Roosevelt handpicked **WILLIAM HOWARD TAFT** to be his successor. Taft promised to continue Roosevelt's agenda, but he was not good at getting new legislation passed or at leading a country. He disliked the job of president, but he did like rich food. During his term in office, he weighed over three hundred pounds and he literally got stuck in the bathtub. Displeased with Taft's performance, Roosevelt formed the "Bull Moose Party" to run against his old friend, which split the vote and cost them both the election. When he left office, Taft became an excellent Supreme Court justice—the job he really wanted. And he lost so much weight that it made the front page of the *New York Times*.

"Politics makes me sick."—W.H.T.

In 1914, when World War I broke out in Europe, **WOODROW WILSON** tried to keep the U.S. out of the conflict. But in 1917, when the Germans sunk the *Lusitania*, a British ship that carried 120 Americans, and then continued to torpedo both British and American ships, Wilson was forced to abandon neutrality. After the war, he proposed a plan that would offer "peace without victory." Its cornerstone was a league of nations where members would gather to settle conflicts. Wilson traveled around the country trying to gain support for his plan. Then he had a stroke, which left him an invalid for the last year of his presidency. The Allies rejected most of Wilson's plan, though they did establish the League of Nations. However, the U.S. did not join it. The League disbanded when it failed to prevent World War II, but when that war ended, fifty countries met to charter a new organization, the United Nations. The U.S. was a founding member.

"If a dog will not come to you after having looked you in the face, you should go home and examine your conscience."—W.W.

WARREN G. HARDING saw the role of president as largely ceremonial. A pro-business conservative, he didn't take strong stands on most issues, although he was publicly in favor of equal rights for African Americans. His wife was much more ambitious. Women had recently received the right to vote, and Florence Harding encouraged them to vote for her husband. Although Harding chose a number of honest, talented men for his cabinet, he also appointed cheats, which led to numerous scandals. Despite being in poor health, Harding decided to take a "Voyage of Understanding" across the country to meet the public, explain his policies, and end the gossip. On the return trip, the exhausted president had a heart attack and died in San Francisco—before he fell out of favor.

"I love to meet people. It is the most pleasant thing I do; it is really the only fun I have. It does not tax me, and it seems to be a very great pleasure to them."—W.G.H.

Nicknamed Silent Cal because he disliked small talk at social events, **CALVIN COOLIDGE** was a somber, thrifty man who liked to sleep a lot. He may have seemed like an odd choice for president during the Roaring Twenties—a period of prosperity, optimism, and partying in underground clubs that sold alcohol, a practice that had been made illegal by Prohibition. Coolidge, who became president when Harding died, won his own election with the slogan "Keeping Cool with Coolidge." Though Coolidge was certainly not solely responsible for the Stock Market Crash of 1929 and the Great Depression that followed, his policies helped lead to these. He promoted easy credit, tax cuts for the wealthy, and reduced regulation for businesses. He did not try to stop feverish speculation (risky investments). Though he was still well liked when he left office, he and his policies became far less popular as the Depression dragged on.

"Perhaps one of the most important accomplishments of my administration has been minding my own business."—C.C.

When **HERBERT HOOVER** took office, he promised more of the same prosperity of the Coolidge years. A skilled administrator who'd organized food relief efforts during and after World War I, Hoover believed that "volunteerism"—cooperation between individuals and groups rather than government intervention—could solve many problems. Though the causes leading to the Depression were already in place by the time Hoover became president, his belief in volunteerism proved unsuccessful at ending it. Although he eventually did establish some public works projects and helped bail out the larger banks, he refused to authorize large-scale financial relief. Homeless Americans forced to live in makeshift shacks took to calling these shantytowns "Hoovervilles." Hoover's name had become a dirty word. In the next presidential election, his opponent won in a landslide.

"In America today, we are nearer a final triumph over poverty than is any other land."—H.H.

At the age of thirty-nine, **FRANKLIN D. ROOSEVELT** suffered from polio, and for the rest of his life he was confined to a wheelchair. The disability did not stop him from becoming governor of New York and then president of the United States. In his inaugural speech, he said, "The only thing we have to fear is fear itself," in reference to the Great Depression. He continued to bolster confidence and calm via the radio through his series of "fireside chats." During his twelve years in office, FDR dealt with the enormous challenges of the Depression and World War II. His "New Deal," which took the Democratic Party in the direction of progressive social programs, involved stabilizing the financial system, offering financial aid, and creating many public works projects. Historians agree that it was the war, which led to the increase in jobs and spending, that finally ended the Depression. Roosevelt did not live to see the decisive victory that brought World War II to its conclusion. But under his leadership, the U.S. rose to become the world's most formidable power.

"I ask you to judge me by the enemies I have made."—F.D.R.

HARRY S. TRUMAN, former haberdasher (owner of a men's clothing store) and U.S. senator, had been vice president for only a short time when Franklin D. Roosevelt died. FDR was a tough act to follow. But Truman was a tough man. He oversaw the end of World War II, making the grim decision to drop atomic bombs on Hiroshima and Nagasaki. To counter the Soviet Union's rise as a world power, he offered aid to anticommunist governments and helped form NATO to protect member nations from outside aggression. When North Korea invaded South Korea, Truman went to South Korea's defense. The resulting Korean War was one that Americans did not fully support or understand. It contributed greatly to the military tension with the Soviet Union and China known as the Cold War—and to Truman's unpopularity. More recently, Truman's stature has improved. He is viewed as a man who truly believed in personal accountability—that the "buck" stopped with him.

"If you can't stand the heat, get out of the kitchen."—H.S.T.

Nicknamed Ike, **DWIGHT D. EISENHOWER** commanded the Allies in Europe during World War II and the NATO forces during the Korean War. As president, he ended the conflict in Korea, yet continued to build up nuclear strength and wage the Cold War. He authorized undercover actions by the Central Intelligence Agency (CIA) to help overthrow unfriendly governments and to support anticommunist leaders. Though he favored a more gradual approach to civil rights issues, he sent federal troops to uphold school desegregation in Little Rock, Arkansas. One of his most important contributions was the Interstate Highway System, which added 41,000 miles of roads across the country. A moderate Republican, he steered a middle path and governed with a "hidden hand": he worked behind the scenes and let his subordinates take the credit for the results—or the blame.

"The middle of the road is all of the usable surface. The extremes, right and left, are in the gutters.—D.D.E.

In 1960, **JOHN F. KENNEDY** challenged his opponent, Richard Nixon, to a series of debates—the first to be shown on television. Looking handsome and relaxed, Kennedy captured the public's attention. He became a symbol of youth, style, and progress, and he won the election. Kennedy's domestic agenda, the "New Frontier," included a variety of social programs, but Congress refused to approve many of them. Kennedy was able to establish the Peace Corps and to set the goal of putting a man on the moon. In foreign affairs, he had to deal with the Cuban Missile Crisis, which brought the U.S. to the brink of nuclear war with the Soviet Union, and with the rising conflict in Vietnam. On November 22, 1963, Kennedy was assassinated as he rode in a motorcade in Dallas, Texas. The response of a horrified, grieving nation was captured on television. To this day, many remain fascinated by the Kennedy presidency and mourn its tragic end.

"If more politicians knew poetry, and more poets knew politics, I am convinced the world would be a little better place in which to live."—J.F.K.

By all accounts, **LYNDON JOHNSON** was a larger-than-life personality, obsessed with earning a place in history. He understood politics, and he knew how to get his way. Sworn in as president after Kennedy's death, the former vice president declared a "War on Poverty," pushed for the late president's social programs, and introduced many of his own, among them environmental protection laws, immigration reform, three civil rights acts, and the establishment of the National Endowment for the Arts, Head Start, Medicaid, and Medicare. Johnson won the 1964 election by a wide margin. But the Vietnam War was intensifying. Johnson escalated it by dropping bombs and sending in half a million troops. As the casualties increased, the antiwar movement grew; and Johnson became the symbol of that terrible and unwinnable war. He chose not to run again and left office a heartbroken man.

"If one morning I walked on top of the water across the Potomac River, the headline that afternoon would read: 'President Can't Swim.'"—L.B.J.

In 1968, **RICHARD NIXON** promised that he would end the Vietnam War. It took five years, during which time Nixon withdrew many troops but stepped up bombings and ordered an invasion of the neighboring country, Cambodia. Yet Nixon, who proposed the Environmental Protection Agency and who helped temporarily stabilize the economy, remained popular, and he was re-elected in 1972 in a landslide. That year he made major achievements in easing tensions with the Soviet Union, and he was the first president to visit China while in office, a trip that met with great public approval. Then came the Watergate scandal, which involved a break-in at Democratic headquarters in the Watergate office building and the subsequent cover-up. During the congressional investigation that followed, Nixon's role in the cover-up was revealed. Before he could be impeached, Nixon resigned—the only president in U.S. history to do so.

"You've got to learn to survive a defeat. That's when you develop character." —R.N.

When Vice President Spiro T. Agnew was forced to resign because of criminal charges, President Nixon chose House minority leader **GERALD FORD** to take his place. Then, after the Watergate scandal, Nixon too resigned, and Ford became president—the only man to achieve that position without the nation's voting him into executive office. He was welcomed as someone who would restore honor to the White House. His inaugural speech declaring, "Our long national nightmare is over," met with nearly universal applause. But when he pardoned Nixon, people became furious. Congress refused to cooperate with him on any of his proposals, and, in 1976, the public refused to elect him to office. Historians have come to view him as a decent man who did indeed try his best to heal a troubled nation.

"I am acutely aware that you have not elected me as your President by your ballots, so I ask you to confirm me with your prayers."—G.F.

JIMMY CARTER, former governor of Georgia, won the candidacy and the election as the outsider who would "clean up the mess in Washington." An honest, hardworking man who supported civil rights and social programs, Carter faced a wide variety of problems, including the hostage crisis—during which Iran captured sixty-six Americans—and the energy crisis caused by oil shortages, which led to long lines at the gas pumps and great frustration among the public. He was blamed for his failure to deal quickly with these crises. A highlight of his presidency was the peace agreement he mediated between Israel and Egypt, two countries that had been at odds for a long time. But that wasn't enough to win Carter a second term. Today, he is known for his work in diplomacy and human rights, making him one of the most respected former presidents of all time.

"Wherever life takes us, there are always moments of wonder."—J.C.

Former actor and spokesperson for General Electric, **RONALD REAGAN** was a Democrat until 1962. He came to believe that the federal government's regulations and taxes were curbing individual freedom and that the U.S. was too soft on the Soviet Union. So he switched parties. As president, he took a hard line against the Soviet Union, which he called an "evil empire," and promoted heavy military buildup. Reagan and fellow Republicans wanted to reduce the size of government. He proposed large tax breaks, which were popular with voters, and he scaled back a number of social programs, yet he greatly increased military spending. The economy faltered, then boomed, but the government's debt continued to mount. To this day, Reagan is viewed by his supporters as one of the greatest presidents and by his detractors as the opposite. Both sides agree that he was a master politician and a force to be reckoned with.

"I know it's hard when you're up to your armpits in alligators to remember you came here to drain the swamp."—R.R.

GEORGE H. W. BUSH already had a long political career before he became the first vice president since Martin Van Buren to be elected president. His posts included ambassador to the United Nations, chairman of the Republican National Committee, and director of the CIA. His strong background in foreign affairs served him well in dealing with the breakup of the Soviet Union and the reunification of Germany when the Berlin Wall was torn down. He was able to put together an international coalition to fight the Persian Gulf War, forcing Saddam Hussein's Iraqi army out of Kuwait. But he didn't fare as well in domestic affairs. During his campaign, he pledged, "Read my lips. No new taxes." However, faced with a large national budget deficit and limited revenue, he broke his promise. Voters chose not to re-elect him for a second term.

"I have opinions of my own, strong opinions, but I don't always agree with them."—G.H.W.B.

Former governor of Arkansas, and saxophone player, **WILLIAM JEFFERSON CLINTON** campaigned as a "New Democrat." He championed both long-held Democratic positions and less traditional ones, such as tough crime laws, free trade with Mexico and Canada, and welfare reform. His economic policies resulted in a large government surplus. In 1995, Clinton vetoed the budget proposed by the Republican-led Congress because it included large cuts to health, educational, and environmental programs. When they failed to reach an agreement, the government shut down. Voters blamed Congress more than Clinton and re-elected him by a wide margin. His second term was marred by a scandal that led to his impeachment, though he was not removed from office and his job approval remained high.

"I like the job. That's what I'll miss the most . . . I'm not sure anybody ever liked this as much as I've liked it."—W.J.C.

Like John Quincy Adams, President **GEORGE W. BUSH** was the son of a former president. His election against Al Gore was highly controversial, involving recounted votes and a Supreme Court decision to determine the final outcome. Bush's main campaign issues were sweeping tax cuts and "No Child Left Behind"—funding for education based on state improvements in reading and math. But then came the September 11, 2001 attacks on New York City's World Trade Center and the Pentagon. The nation and much of the world supported the president and his War on Terror, which focused on attempts to capture mastermind Osama bin Laden, and to destroy terrorist groups based in Afghanistan. Then Bush decided to invade Iraq, where he believed that the leader Saddam Hussein was hiding "weapons of mass destruction." The war proved to be costly and led to a large government deficit. Bush left office with low approval among voters.

"The true history of my administration will be written fifty years from now, and you and I will not be around to see it."—G.W. B.

Illinois senator **BARACK OBAMA** made history by becoming our first black president. In his campaign, he promised change. The U.S. was involved in long wars in Iraq and Afghanistan and was in a serious recession caused by reckless mortgage lending, deregulation, and other factors. Obama ran on a platform of ending the wars, stimulating the economy, weaning the country from dependence on foreign oil, and offering healthcare for all. During his first term, he proposed healthcare reform, which was passed by Congress, cut taxes for working families and small businesses, signed a stimulus bill, withdrew troops from Iraq, and ordered the operation that captured and killed Osama bin Laden. Facing a nation divided by political ideology and partisanship, Obama was re-elected in 2012. His first major issues were immigration reform, gun control, climate change, and the federal budget—all of which have continued to be challenging issues for our times.

"None of us wants to be defined by just one part of what makes us whole."—B.O.

SOURCES

For research, I read many books and articles and watched a number of excellent documentaries, in particular a series on the History Channel (*The Presidents*) and one on PBS (*American Experience: The Presidents*). Here are a few other sources:

BOOKS

Our White House: Looking in, Looking Out. Cambridge, Massachusetts: Candlewick Press, 2008.

Carter, Graydon, editor. *Vanity Fair's Presidential Profiles*. New York: Abrams, 2010.

Davis, Kenneth C. *Don't Know Much About the Presidents*. New York: HarperCollins, 2002.

O'Brien, Cormac. *Secret Lives of the U.S. Presidents*, Philadelphia: Quirk Books, 2009.

O'Connor, Jane. *If the Walls Could Talk: Family Life at the White House*, New York: Simon & Schuster, 2004.

Strock, Ian Randal. *The Presidential Book of Lists*. New York: Villard Books, 2008.

WEBSITES

www.history.com/topics/the-us-presidents

www.millercenter.org

www.pbs.org/wgbh/americanexperience/collections/presidents

www.potus.com

www.presidentsusa.net

www.whitehouse.gov